W9-CJN-466

Nabulela

A South African Folk Tale

Retold and illustrated by
FIONA MOODIE

Farrar, Straus and Giroux · New York

THERE WAS ONCE a deep, deep lake in Africa. In the lake
lived a white-skinned monster called Nabulela. Nabulela, the
monster that ate people.

Not far from the lake was a kraal. To keep Nabulela peaceful, the people of the village would take flat cakes to the lake every evening at sunset. They would put the cakes down at the edge of the water and sing:

"*Nabulela, Nabulela, come out and eat me.*"

Then they would run away as fast as they could, back to the kraal.

Now, the chief of the kraal was very sad because he had only sons. At last, a baby daughter was born to him. He called her Nandi and he was very proud of her.

There was feasting for many days at the birth of the baby girl.

Nandi grew up to be beautiful and kind, but the chief, her father, spoiled her with necklaces and ornaments. He was always singing her praises.

The other girls her age were jealous when they saw all the gifts she was given, and they began to hate her, although they were careful to hide their hatred.

One day when Nandi was seven years old, she was playing a little way from the other girls near the river. She suddenly cried out. She could see a little paw waving from the water.

The others laughed, but Nandi scrambled down the riverbank to reach the creature.

It was a puppy. Someone had tried to drown him, but Nandi saved him and took him home with her.

"I shall call you Bubhezi," said Nandi to the puppy, "because now you are small and weak but one day you will be big and brave – like a lion!"

She fed him and looked after him and he followed her everywhere.

Three years went by and Bubhezi, now a grown dog, still went everywhere with Nandi, and she was glad to have him at her side.

One day when Nandi was about ten years old, the girls her age were sent to fetch clay from the clay pit quite far from the kraal. Their mothers needed the clay to make pots.

Bubhezi was tied up that day, as Nandi didn't want him to
fall into the deep clay pit.

On the way to the pit, the girls passed the elephant rocks.
"Let's climb up there," they whispered to one another.
"Maybe Nandi will fall down the gap!" they said, giggling.
Nandi didn't hear them.

They all climbed up to the top of the rocks and one by one jumped over the gap. When Nandi's turn came, the girls behind gave her a push. She slipped and fell down, down, down into the hole at the bottom of the rocks.

"Where is Nandi?" the villagers asked when the girls came home with the clay.

"Oh, she went back to find one of her bangles. It must have got caught on a branch," said the girls.

As darkness fell, faithful Bubhezi chewed through the thong that bound him and ran off to look for his mistress. He found her crying in the hole at the bottom of the elephant rocks. She threw her dog one of her bangles.

"Take this to my father, Bubhezi," she called.

On the way home, Bubhezi met a search party of men with torches.

"Take us to Nandi," the men said, when they saw her bangle in the dog's mouth.

Bubhezi turned and ran back to the rocks.

Lions were gathering hungrily above the hole where Nandi
huddled.

"U, U, U!" shouted the men and waved their flaming torches.
The lions ran away and the men helped Nandi out of the pit
and took her home.

The next morning, the chief spoke fiercely to the young girls.
"You have been very wicked," he bellowed. "I should send
you away from the kraal into the bush. I should banish you
forever. But I shall give you one chance. If you bring me the
skin of Nabulela – Nabulela, who lives in the lake – I shall
forgive you. Now go from my sight."

The girls trembled.

"How can we do this thing?" they asked one another. At last they made a plan and spoke to their fathers and brothers. Then they ground some corn and made flat cakes. At sunset they walked fearfully down to the lake – the lake of Nabulela – carrying with them the cakes.

When they came to the edge of the lake, the girls put down
the cakes, first one, then the next a little farther away, until
there was a long trail of cakes to tempt the monster out of
the lake.

Then the girls sang:
      "Nabulela, Nabulela, come out and eat me!
      Nabulela, Nabulela, come out and eat me!"
They hovered at the edge of the lake until the monster heaved itself out of the water. Then they ran.

The monster swallowed the cakes one by one.

"Nabulela! Nabulela!" taunted the girls, just ahead of the last cake. Enraged by their impudence, Nabulela began to chase them. He was angry and still hungry. The girls ran and ran, always keeping just out of his reach.

The monster chased them up the hill, over the rocks, all the way to the kraal. The fathers and brothers were waiting for Nabulela. When he entered the kraal, two of the girls shut the gate so he couldn't escape.

The men fell on him with their assegais and soon Nabulela
lay dead. Nabulela, the dreadful monster, feared for many
years.

They skinned him and put the skin to dry in the sun. When
the skin was ready, the girls took it to the chief.

The chief put on the skin of Nabulela and this is what he said:
"You have been very brave, my girls. I thank you for the skin
of the monster. You have helped to rid our people of Nabulela
forever. I forgive you the wickedness you did to Nandi. But I
see now that I, too, did wrong always to favor my daughter over
you. Henceforth, I shall treat you all equally."

From that day, Nandi and the other girls lived together as
friends and Bubhezi was loved and praised for the rest of his days.

For Sean

First published in Great Britain by Andersen Press Ltd., 1996

Color separations by Photolitho AG, Zurich, Switzerland

Printed and bound in Italy by Grafiche AZ, Verona

First American edition, 1997

Library of Congress Cataloging-in-Publication Data

Moodie, Fiona.

Nabulela / Fiona Moodie. — 1st American ed.

p.   cm.

[1. Nguni (African people)—Folklore.   2. Folklore—South Africa.]   I. Title.

PZ8.1.M775Nab   1997   398.2'08996398—dc20   96–27938   CIP   AC